Mrs Wobble the Waitress

by ALLAN AHLBERG

with pictures by
JANET AHLBERG

Puffin

Viking

PUFFIN/VIKING

Published by the Penguin Group
Penguin Books Ltd, 27 Wrights Lane, London W8 5TZ, England
Penguin Books USA Inc., 375 Hudson Street, New York, New York 10014, USA
Penguin Books Australia Ltd, Ringwood, Victoria, Australia
Penguin Books Canada Ltd, 10 Alcorn Avenue, Toronto, Ontario, Canada M4V 3B2
Penguin Books (NZ) Ltd, 182–190 Wairau Road, Auckland 10, New Zealand

Penguin Books Ltd, Registered Offices: Harmondsworth, Middlesex, England

First published 1988
21 23 25 27 29 30 28 26 24 22

Text copyright © Allan Ahlberg, 1988
Illustrations copyright © Janet Ahlberg, 1988

Educational Advisory Editor: Brian Thompson

All rights reserved.
Without limiting the rights under copyright
reserved above, no part of this publication may be
reproduced, stored in or introduced into a retrieval system,
or transmitted, in any form or by any means (electronic, mechanical,
photocopying, recording or otherwise), without the prior
written permission of both the copyright owner and
the above publisher of this book

Printed and bound in Great Britain by
William Clowes Limited, Beccles and London
Set in Century Schoolbook by Filmtype Services Limited, Scarborough

ISBN Paperback 0 14 03.1239 0
ISBN Hardback 0-670-80577-7

Mrs Wobble was a waitress.
She liked her work.
The customers liked her.
The only trouble was – she wobbled.

One day Mrs Wobble wobbled
with a bowl of soup.
The soup landed on a
customer's dog.
Mrs Wobble got told off.

The next day Mrs Wobble wobbled
with a roast chicken.
The roast chicken landed
on a customer's head.
Mrs Wobble got told off again.

The next day Mrs Wobble wobbled
with a plate of jelly.
The jelly landed on the
manager's head.
Mrs Wobble got the sack.

Mrs Wobble went home to her family.
Mr Wobble cooked her tea.
The children tried to cheer her up.
"Cheer up, Ma!" they said.
"You will find another job –
in another café!"

But there were no other cafés.
That was the only one in the town.
Mrs Wobble knew this.
"There are no other cafés,"
she said.
And she began to cry.

The children did not like
to see their mother cry.
It made them cry.
It made their father cry too.

Then Mr Wobble had an idea.
"I know what we can do," he said.
"We can open a café of our own."

"Where?" said Mrs Wobble.
"Where?" said Miss Wobble.
"Where?" said Master Wobble.
"Here!" said Mr Wobble.
"We can turn the house into a café!"

The next day the Wobble family
turned their house into a café.
They cleaned and painted.

They moved the chairs
and tables around.
They changed the curtains.

Mr Wobble went shopping.
He bought meat and vegetables,
fruit and fish,
cheese and chicken,
flour and a few other things.

The children went shopping too.
They bought two pairs of roller-skates
and a fishing net.
"What are those for?" said Mr Wobble.
"It's a surprise, Pa,"
the children said.
"You wait and see!"

In the evening Mrs Wobble made
waiter's clothes for her children,
and a cook's hat for her husband.

Mr Wobble and the children
made the menus.

The children went to bed.
Mr and Mrs Wobble stepped outside.
They looked at their new café.
"It's the big day, tomorrow,"
Mr Wobble said.
"We are going to make our fortunes."
"Yes," said Mrs Wobble.
"The only trouble is –
what if I wobble?"

The next day the children woke up early.
"It's the big day, today, Ma,"
Master Wobble said.
He gave his mother
a cup of tea in bed.
Miss Wobble gave her father
a cup of tea in bed.
"We are going to make our fortunes
today, Pa," she said.

After breakfast
Mr Wobble began cooking.

Mrs Wobble
and Miss Wobble
laid the tables.

Master Wobble
went round the town
with a sandwich-board.

Eat at Wobbles Cosy Cafe

The first customers arrived.
"Oh dear," said Mrs Wobble.
"What if I . . . ?"

Mrs Wobble wobbled
with a bowl of soup.
"Help!" said the customer.
Miss Wobble skated to the rescue.
She caught the soup in another bowl.
"That's clever!" the customer said.

Mrs Wobble wobbled
with a roast chicken.
"Wow!" said the customer.
Master Wobble skated to the rescue.
He caught the roast chicken
in a net.
"Hooray!" the customer said.

Then all the other customers cheered.
"Hooray, hooray!"
"This is more fun than a circus!"
they said.

That night Mrs Wobble counted the money.
"It looks like a fortune to us, Ma,"
the children said.
Mr Wobble gave them a hug.
"And we owe it all to the
famous juggling waiters!" he said.

The next day there was a big crowd
in the street.
The people had come from miles around
to see the famous juggling waiters.

The children peeped out.
"There's a big crowd in the
street, Ma," they said.
"Yes," said Mrs Wobble.
And she began to laugh.
"Now the only trouble is –
what if I *don't* wobble?"

The End